THE SCOLIOSAURUS

Written and Illustrated by
Lauren Davis

These hand and footprints were taken from you on the
5th of February 2021

This book is dedicated to my most wished for gift and wonderful little boy, Jesse - James.

Mammy loves you more than life sweetheart.

I wanted to make this dinosaur obsessed part of your life more prominent than it already is, to help you and I remember the happy times when you were just a baby.

All my love, Mammy. xxx

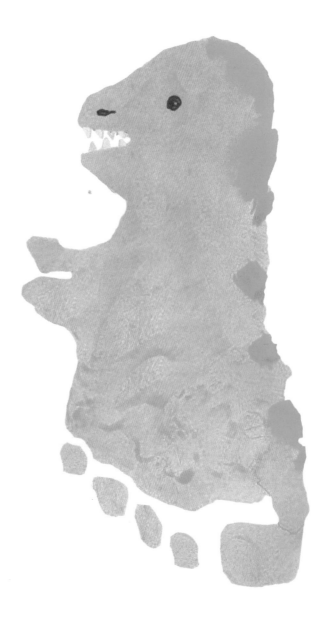

ON A BEAUTIFUL BUSY MORNING IN THE MIDDLE OF SPRING SONNY THE TYRANNOSAUR WAS BORN

SONNY CAME FROM A LONG LINE OF STRONG AND RESPECTED TYRANNOSAURS

HIS FAMILY WAS VERY PROUD OF
BEING THE MOST FAMOUS DINOSAUR
THERE EVER WAS

BEING DIFFERENT IS WHAT
MAKES LIFE MORE FUN THEY
ALL USED TO SAY

HIS BEST FRIEND WAS A FROG
NAMED JESSE WHO WAS
THERE ON THE VERY DAY HE
WAS BORN

SONNY AND HIS FRIENDS
LOVED SCIENCE CLASS
WITH MR RAPTORIAN

THEY LOVED
LEARNING
ABOUT BONES
AND HOW
DINOSAURS
B O D I E S
WORKED

ONE DAY SONNYS
SPINE STARTED TO
HURT HIM ASWELL
AS HIS BIG FEET AND
HE FELT OUT OF
BREATHE ALL OF
THE TIME

THIS WAS NOT
GOOD FOR A
TYRANNOSAUR

SONNY TRIED TO IGNORE IT UNTIL HIS FRIENDS POINTED OUT THAT HIS SHOULDERS WERE OFF BALANCE

OTHER TYRANNOSAUR KIDS DID NOT UNDERSTAND WHAT WAS GOING ON WITH SONNY AND STARTING TO MAKE FUN OF HIM

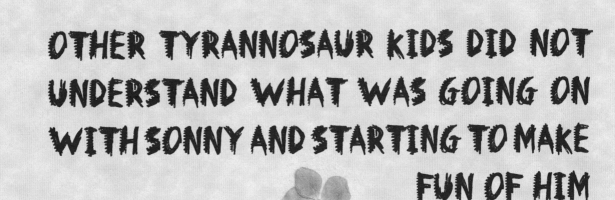

WHEN HE GOT HOME THAT NIGHT HE TOLD HIS PARENTS AND THEY WERE SHOCKED AT HOW THE OTHER KIDS ACTED

HOWEVER SONNYS PARENTS FOR PEACE OF MIND BELIEVED THEY SHOULD TAKE HIM TO THE DOCTORS

SONNY WAS TAKEN TO SEE DR PTERANODOC
THE BEST DOCTOR IN ALL OF THE VALLEY

WHO TOLD SONNY HE HAD **SCOLIOSIS**
ALL OF THE TYRANNOSAUR FAMILY WERE SHOCKED

DR PTERANODOC TOLD THE FAMILY
TO FIX SONNYS SPINE
SONNY WOULD HAVE TO
HAVE AN OPERATION

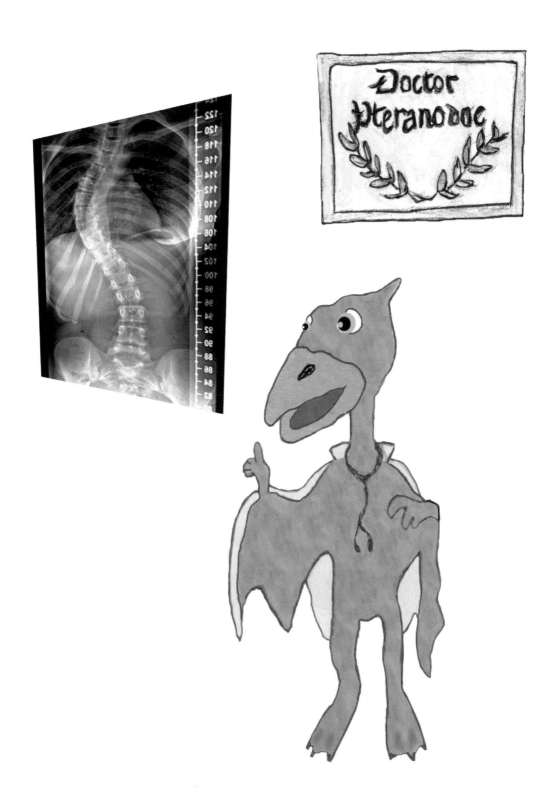

THE FAMILY AND SONNY THOUGHT LONG
AND HARD BUT KNEW THAT THE BEST THING
FOR SONNY WAS TO HAVE THE OPERATION

SONNY SPOKE TO HIS FRIENDS
ABOUT IT AND THEY ALL TOLD
HIM WHATEVER HIS
DECISION WAS THEY WOULD
ALWAYS BE HIS FRIEND AND
THERE TO SUPPORT HIM

WHATEVER SONNY LOOKED
LIKE DID NOT MATTER TO
HIS FRIENDS AS THEY SAID
DIFFERENT WAS GOOD

SONNYS BEST FRIEND JESSE THE FROG WAS A PINK FROG AND ALL OF HIS FAMILY WERE A GREENY BLUE COLOUR AND HIS FAMILY NEVER UNDERSTOOD HOW JESSE WAS THAT COLOUR BUT STILL LOVED HIM

SONNYS GOOD FRIEND BENNY THE BRACHIOSAURUS WAS A SHORT BRACHIOSAURUS THIS WAS NOT COMMON IN THIS TYPE OF DINOSAUR AS THEY WERE NORMALLY SO TALL BUT BENNYS FAMILY STILL LOVED HIM

SONNYS GOOD FRIEND TOMMY THE
TRICERATOPS DID NOT HAVE A NOSE
HORN IT WAS NOT COMMON FOR
THIS TYPE OF DINOSAUR TO NOT
HAVE A NOSE HORN BUT TOMMYS
FAMILY STILL LOVED HIM

SONNYS GOOD FRIEND SCARLETT
THE STEGOSAURUS HAD ONE EYE
MISSING SHE LOOKED LIKE SHE
MUST OF BEEN IN AN EPIC BATTLE
BUT SHE COULD SEE JUST AS WELL
AS EVERYONE ELSE BUT SCARLETTS
FAMILY STILL LOVED HER

WHAT SONNY
LEARNT FROM THIS
LOOKING AROUND AT HIS FRIENDS WITH WHAT HE
HAD WITH HIS SCOLIOSIS IS THAT THE PEOPLE WHO
CARE FOR YOU WILL STILL LOVE YOU IT DOES NOT
MATTER IF YOU ARE DIFFERENT FROM
EVERYBODY ELSE

WHAT SONNY FINALLY DECIDED WAS TO HAVE THE SCOLIOSIS OPERATION AND HE KNEW IT WAS GOING TO BE HARD TO GO THROUGH BUT IT WOULD MAKE HIS LIFE SO MUCH BETTER

THE DAY OF THE SURGERY CAME AND SONNY WAS
GOING TO BE SENT DOWN TO THEATRE
TO BE PUT TO SLEEP AND WHEN HE WOULD
WAKE UP HE WOULD HAVE A STRAIGHT SPINE
AND BE IN NO MORE PAIN

COUNT DOWN TO 3 2 1 AND
YOU WILL BE ASLEEP
SAID DR PTERANODOC

SONNY HAD HIS OPERATION AND
WAS A VERY BRAVE DINOSAUR

HE WAS RESTING NOW ON A
NEST WAITING TO
RECOVER FROM HIS BIG
SURGERY

WHEN HE WOULD WAKE UP
HIS FAMILY AND FRIENDS
WOULD BE THERE

WHEN HE WOKE UP HIS FRIENDS
AND FAMILY WERE
SO PROUD OF HOW BRAVE
SONNY WAS AND TOLD
HIM AGAIN THEY WOULD LOVE
HIM NO MATTER WHAT

NOW SONNY COULD STAND UP HE WAS
ALLOWED TO LOOK AT HIS COOL SCAR

WOW SAID HIS FRIENDS AND FAMILY
YOU LOOK LIKE YOU HAVE SURVIVED AN
EPIC BATTLE AND NOW YOU HAVE THE SCAR
TO PROVE IT

JESSE THE FROG THEN POINTED OUT THAT
SONNY IS A SCOLIOSAUR

THE FIRST EVER
SCOLIOSAURUS

SONNY HAD ALL GROWN UP NOW AND LOVED
THE WAY HE HAD NO MORE PAIN JUST A
COOL SCAR DOWN HIS SPINE

NO OTHER DINOSAUR WOULD CROSS HIS
PATH AS SONNY WAS KNOWN AS THE
BRAVEST DINOSAUR WHO EVER LIVED

SONNY THE T REX FINDS STRENGTH
IN HIS JOURNEY THROUGH LIFE
WITH SCOLIOSIS WITH THE HELP OF
HIS BEST FRIENDS AND FAMILY

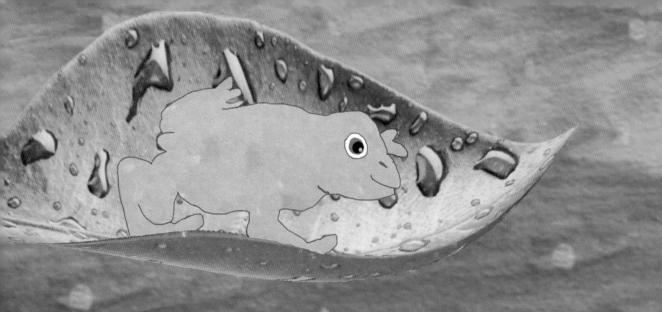

SONNYS BEST FRIEND JESSE WAS
ALWAYS THERE TO WATCH HIM FROM AFAR

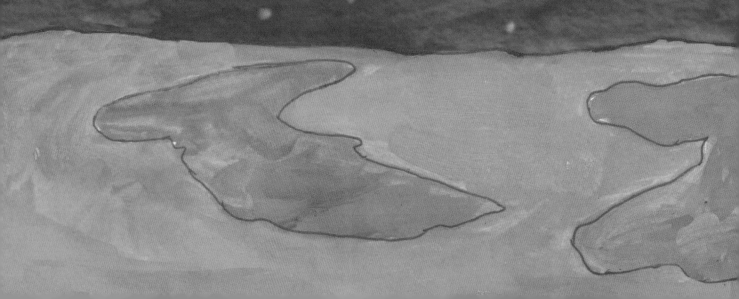

THE BRAVEST DINOSAUR THERE EVER WAS